Where the Socks Go

Written By:
Claudine Barbot
Jocelyne Barbot
Nicole Green McCalla

DEDICATIONS AND ACKNOWLEDGEMENTS

Thanks always to God,

And to our families for the undying support and encouragement. We thank you.

We dedicate this book to children and the young at heart all over the world

Who appreciate imagination and the written word.

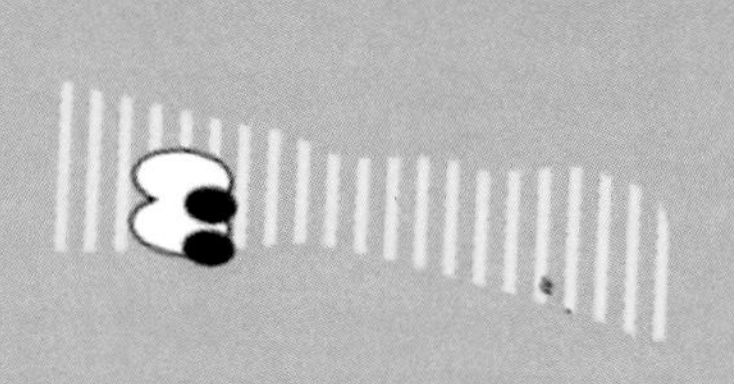

Do your socks ever go missing?
And you search high and low
But no matter how much you look,
You just don't know where they go.

And your mommy keeps fussing
But you know it's not you,
Because you put them in pairs
Like she told you to do.

And days turn to months,
And sometimes months turn to years,
Then you forget all about them
And just like that they appear.

Some days in the laundry
Or maybe under your bed,
And you sit and you look
While scratching your head.

"But I looked there ten times
Or maybe a hundred or more,
And I promise you,
There was no sock there before."

It's more than just weird—
Those socks are sneaky, you know...
This book tells the story of
Where the Socks Go...

Laundry Day

In the back of the dryer, in the curve to the right,
There is a door flap that is way out of your sight.

And every so often, but not all of the time,
A few of your socks venture inside.

There are rules to this routine: don't all go at once!
So the sock owners don't get too much of a hunch.

Some days it's the left socks, others the right.
But you can never quite guess it, try as you might.

And it all starts in the basket when mommy puts them all in,
That's when the scheming and plotting begins.

All socks are in on it, from whites to the colors—
Even the fancy ones with the designs and the flowers.

They all jump into the washer so they can get fresh,
They can't go to the sock world a stinky sock mess.

Next phase is the dryer, where the magic is done.
Some enter as two and leave out as one.

How they decide it, we'll never quite know.
What matters however, is where the socks go.

When the dryer is no longer in view,
And there's only one left of what used to be two.

They fall from the sky and float through the air,
Then they are scanned to make sure they are no longer in pairs.

Next, left socks go right and right socks go left.
Just to keep order… Can't risk a sock mess.

And what happens next is unexpected, I say!
The socks are released so they can go play.

Yes! They have sock slides and sock roller coasters,
Sock swings, sock things, and even sock posters.

It's a fun world for socks! Sock Land, it is called.
Visited by a few, but loved by all.

Meanwhile, back home, the dryer is finished.
And just like that, my sock's pairs have vanished.

Mommy can't find the green one or the blue one with stripes.
She looks everywhere, but they are nowhere in sight.

Then she says "Johnny, you've done it once more!
Your socks are still missing just like before!"

"But, Mommy," I say. "Oh stop, that's enough!
Since you can't keep them in pairs, I'll stop buying socks!"

"But, my feet will be cold. I'll find them, you'll see.
I really put them in pairs just like you told me."

So I go on a hunt for the socks that are missing.
I look everywhere—even the kitchen.

Still, I can't find the green one or the blue one with stripes.
All of my socks remain out of sight.

So I go to the dryer, and pop my head in,
Looking for something... anything!

No socks in the dryer, but wait—something just wiggled,
And I think I just heard a few giggles.

No, that's impossible, I'm going upstairs.
Maybe I'll find something there...

Not under the couch, or tucked in the cushions.
I'm not giving up until I finish this mission.

Okay, I am beat! I've looked all around...
Wait what's that? Look what I've found!

The socks that were missing... every last one.
Wait until I show mommy what I have done.

There's one on my dresser and the edge of my bed
And another one just fell on my head.

I'll grab them and show her. Just wait until she sees!
Then she'll stop being so angry with me.

So I go to grab them and they just disappear.
But, that can't be, they were just here!

Is this some type of a trick? I don't understand.
How did this happen? Who thought up this plan?

And there goes the laughter… I just heard some giggles.
And across the room, I saw something wiggle.

This is getting a bit scary and my socks are still gone.
I don't know what's happening, but something is wrong.

I go to tell mommy, and she comes running quick
And I explain to her the naughty sock trick.

"Mommy, I told you! It's really not me.
The socks, it's the socks! Come so you'll see,"

"Johnny, this is silly! Socks don't play jokes.
Is this to make me forget? Is this some type of hoax?"

"No Mom, it's true! I had the blue sock with stripes
And even the green one was right in my sight."

And all of a sudden they vanished and giggled.
And I promise you, I saw them all wiggle.

“Look there, on the edge of my bed!
That’s where I saw it and there was one on my head!”

“Johnny, stop being silly. Your socks are all here.
I need to wash them, so take them downstairs.”

And there they all were, every last sock:
The green one, the white one, and the blue one with stripes.

One on my dresser, and one on the edge of my bed,
And even the one that fell on my head.

So I grabbed them all tight and examined them close.
Put them with their pair so there were no more jokes.

And later that evening, I would hear mommy call.
“Johnny, where are your socks? I can’t find them at all!”

Flying High

In my pretty pink tutu,
I place my socks in a row.

The frilly pink kind I wear on Sundays,
You know.

And I practice my spins
And my jumps; up and down.

In the background, there's a sock
Spinning and twirling around.

Just like her owner, the sock
Leaps here and there.

Dancing and prancing around everywhere.
And all of a sudden, from the open window nearby...

There's a gust of wind that sends the sock flying high.

She whirls through the air with her fancy designs.

She soars through the clouds with no fear of flying.

She follows the wind gracefully all the way to the ground.

And she takes several bows when she's finally down.

Meanwhile, in her room, Sally finally stops spinning.
Only to notice that one of her socks has gone missing.

She looks around puzzled. "But, it was just there on my bed!"
She looks around again quickly while scratching her head.

Then she drops to her knees and looks under all things.
She checks under her sheets and in her toy bins.

Her room is so messy now— toys everywhere!

And her sock is still gone... It just isn't there.

Down in the grass, her sock is having great fun...
Doing things socks do when we are looking for one.

Sally sits crying. That was her favorite pink pair
To think she can't find her sock anywhere...

And what about mother? What will she say?
When she finds out what happened today?

Sally goes to her window and begins sobbing.
And below her, her sock is relaxing and lounging.

"Where is my sock?" Sally screams while she cries.
“That sock is my favorite; of all the socks I have...Why?”

While she cries, her sock is enjoying the town.
Sightseeing and such as she prances around.

But she hears Sally's sobbing and she stops in her tracks,
And finds herself slowly traveling back.
Just then, the wind blows.
And it's up, up, and away!

And the sock soars through the sky,
Still pirouetting and doing ballet.

And with another strong gust,
She lands right beside Sally

Who's still sniffling and crying
And complaining so sadly.

"Now what will I do? No other sock is so right."
"And that one fit perfect—not too loose, not too tight."

She reaches for a tissue, but grabs her sock in its place,
Bringing it carelessly up to her face.

The sock jumps out of her hand and drops to the floor.
"But, wait! It's my sock... it was not there before!"

She grabs it and hugs it and spins all around.
"Oh, my sock. My sweet sock! How I looked up and down."

Meanwhile, the other socks giggle because they saw the whole thing unfold.
And poor Sally is so happy, but does not even know.

Suddenly, she stops and she thinks. "Did you jump out of my hand?
You did. You had to! But, I don't understand!"

She drops the sock quickly, but it lies limp on the floor.
She stares at it closely and pokes it to examine it more.

Then out of nowhere, she hears a soft giggling.
She turns quick just to see something wiggling.

"What's going on? I'm always alone in this room.
But something seems strange in here this afternoon."

When she turns back around, her sock has vanished—it's true!
And she let's out a yelp when she notices her sock is now two.

"You were just on the floor. I know because I left you right there.
But now you are on the bed together with your pair?"

She stops and she thinks for a while.
And that's when it happens! Her sock gives her a smile.

"Mommy! Mommy! Come quick!
Something is wrong! I think I am sick!"

Her mother comes running, and Sally tells her the tale,
And mom gives her "the stare" and tells her that cannot be real.

Mom walks away and Sally sits stumped on her bed,
And she reaches for her sock, but it is missing again.

Hidden Below

"I'll be down as soon as I find my polka dot sock.
Go on to the car. I'll remember the lock."

"Hmmm, where can that sock be? I left it right here—
Right there on the floor. It has to be near."

"Maybe it's under my laundry... This room is a mess.
Or maybe it's where I last got undressed."

"I have to be quick now so mom won't be mad.
They're waiting for me in the car—her and dad."

Meanwhile down below, he is under the bed.
You know, the polka dot sock, like the little boy said.

Down below he is hiding, ducking down behind shoes,
Hiding and playing like naughty socks do.

He jumps out of one shoe and into the other,
Skipping about without any bothers.

On the other hand, Bobby is losing his mind,
Fretting over the sock he can't find.

And mommy and daddy are tired of waiting.
They've tried, but they can no longer be patient.

So mom marches inside. "Young man, how long can it possibly take?
It's only one sock, for goodness sake!"

"Mom, I am looking, but it's hiding, I know.
I put it right there, but where did it go?"

"Bobby, socks are not living. So that's silly, you see.
I'll find it myself. You leave it to me."

Mom stomps up the stairs with her face steaming red.
"I bet you it's lost in the mess under your bed."

"And if I can't find it, I want you to know,
You're wearing another so we can just go."

"But Mom! That's my favorite. It's lucky, I say!
If I don't wear it, I'll lose today."

Hearing what the little boy said,
The polka dot sock comes from under the bed.

He sneaks by some shoes and a purple sock hiding,
And on his way out, he sees more socks smiling.

He jumps out gently and lands on the floor
So Bobby won't have to look anymore.

When mom enters the room she takes a deep sigh…
"Bobby, your room's a disaster. Oh my!"

"Mom, it doesn't matter, my sock is still gone.
Let's just go so we can hurry back home."

"Look! There's your sock Bobby, right there under your bed.
I promise if it wasn't stuck tight, you might lose your head."

"Mommy, I looked there like ten times or more.
That sock was not right there on the floor."

Bobby just stood there, shocked for a while.
He just stared at his sock and the sock seemed to smile.

"Mom, did you see that? My sock it just smiled,
It will do it, I promise, if you just stare for a while!"

"Oh Bobby, you're silly. It would be cute if it did.
I had the same imagination when I was a kid.

Now go get your things, we are going to be late.
And hurry, you know dad does not like to wait."

And off the boy went still puzzled a bit.
He picked up the sock and just stared at it.

No smiles—nothing. It was still as can be.
"I saw this sock smile. I know it's not me."

He stuffed the sock in his bag deep and far down as can be.

"Oh well, I better get moving, just like mom said."
And just then, the sock's twin leaped back under the bed...

Between the Sheets

"Goodnight Daddy!" I'm all snug in my sheets,
Waiting patiently to fall sound asleep.

I have on my yellow pajamas with the blue dots,
And to match, daddy put on my fuzzy yellowish socks.

I'm so warm in my bed and I can feel my eyes falling asleep.
But something keeps happening beneath my sheets.

There's a draft on my ankle. Where did my sock go?
It's in the sheets somewhere. That I know.

I turn on my flashlight and cover my head,
Shining the light all over my bed.

Well, that's funny, my sock isn't here.
I've only been in bed, so it has to be near.

"What is that moving?" Angie dives to the edge of her bed.
Then suddenly, the figure zooms past her head.

"Am I going crazy?" She shines her light quick.
"Something flew past me. Or at least, that's what I think."

But my sock is still missing. Wait, there it goes again!
And again, and again, and again, and again!

Angie keeps looking, but this something is fast.
Left, now right. It keeps flying past.

"Okay, little something, I surrender, I quit!
Just show yourself and that'll be it."

Instead she hears giggles and she starts to get scared.
"What is so funny? Tell me, who's there?"

Then it all stops—both the movement and giggles.
And she puts her head down, but then something wiggles!

"Daddy. Oh Daddy! Come rescue me now!
Someone, something's in my bed. I don't know who or how!"

Daddy comes running. "Angie, you had a nightmare—it's just you and I.
It was only a dream. You don't have to cry."

"Daddy, I know that you checked, but that's crazy, I say!
I saw it, I heard it. Please don't go away."

"Look Honey, I'm working. You just had a bad dream,
But that can be scary so I know what you mean."

"No, Daddy, I didn't. I was awake all along!
You have to believe me. I know I'm not wrong."

"Here's what we'll do. I'll leave the door cracked.
That way you can see me and I'll keep checking back."

Then daddy left and Angie sat there afraid,
Wishing so hard that her daddy had stayed.

After a minute, or ten minutes, or more,
Angie's eyes were heavy, just like before.

Just as she dozed, something tickled her toes.
And ran up beside her, tickling her nose.

She grabbed for her flashlight, but nothing was there—
Not a person or thing in sight anywhere.

So she peeked from under the covers and wanting to play,
That fuzzy yellowish sock went the other way.

Finally! She caught a glimpse. "No, It can't be!
It looks like my sock is hiding from me."

With that came a giggle and Angie caught it, she did!
But with a swift wiggle, the sock broke free from that kid.

"Come back here!" Angie called, getting twisted under the covers.
But that yellowish sock just kept running all over.

Angie went up and the sock ran back down,
They did that back and forth until they ran all around.

"I'll pretend to be asleep... That should do the trick!
Then he will stop, and I will snatch him up quick."

So she closed her eyes and did not move one bit,
And that yellowish sock—well, he fell for it.

When he came close, she snatched him just like she said
And put him back on her foot and then went to bed.

All warm once again, Angie dozed off rather swiftly,
And morning came just as quickly.

She sat up smiling and stretched and yawned,
And looked down at her foot... Her sock was gone!

She looked under the covers and it was not there.
She could not find it anywhere!

"Oh well, one sock is better than none.
I'll miss that yellowish sock. He was really quite fun."

And when that sock heard her, he finally appeared.
"Hey, it's right there under my pillow. I knew it was near!"

Sock Monster

"He's at it again. Look down at your feet.
And it's not just because your side is not neat.

That monster! He does it when you are asleep.
He pulls off your sock and has a sock feast!"

"Ryan, please, I can't take it!
The sock is just lost in this room.

I bet it'll show up pretty soon."

"Bryan, that's crazy! Socks don't just go missing.
That monster is eating them. I just wish you would listen!"

"So you're telling me that when I am sound asleep,
Some monster comes up and plays with my feet?

But he doesn't eat me, because he'd rather have socks?
I don't buy it at all, I really do not!"

"Bryan, just think, my socks are all in one place,
But look at the difference... I have a neat space.

Your side is all messy, like a monster's room would be.
That's why he eats your socks and doesn't touch me."

Meanwhile in the closet, the monster is listening,
Wondering how Ryan knows all of his business.

The socks are all giggling
Because the monster is their friend.

The boy thinks he eats them
But he's nice instead.

ZZZZ

Late in the evening, when the boys are asleep,
The socks and the monster play hide-and-go-seek.

And they always choose Bryan because he has so many places to hide.
Ryan doesn't have much on his side.

They hide under his blanket and behind all of his toys,
They're always so careful, so they don't wake the boys.

Sometimes, that Ryan will wake up in a flash,
And the socks and the monster have to run away fast.

The socks dive behind anything—a pile of laundry or a shoe.
And the monster—well, he always hides too.

Then they sit and they wait until Ryan starts snoring.
It takes forever some nights... It's really quite boring.

And finally, when their game is all done,
After they've hid every possible place and have had all that fun

It's time to go back and the monster is so silly.
He always pulls Bryan's sock off, for no reason really.

And then there goes Ryan staring at Bryan's bare toes,
Wondering where his sock always goes.

So one day, finally, Ryan comes up with a plan.
"I know it's that monster. I just don't understand.

So I'll stay up all night and I'll catch him, you'll see!
I'll teach him not to mess with my brother or me."

Night came and all camped out in his bed,
Ryan sat with his binoculars and flashlight in hand.

And after two hours, or three, or more,
He thought he was crazy when something opened the door.

It was fuzzy and green with socks for hands,
And he froze in place... He couldn't remember his plan.

He tried to wake Bryan, but he wouldn't move,
So he sat there frozen that night in his room.

Behind the monster, the socks were all giggling
And smiling and such, while some others were wiggling.

And Ryan finally parted his lips.
"Mommy, Mommy! Please come quick!"

Mommy came running. "Ryan what's wrong?"
Ryan just pointed and stared at the wall.

"Baby, there's nothing there. Did you have a bad dream?
I think so. At least that's what it seems."

"No, that's not it! There was a monster, I swear!
He was smiling and happy and standing right over there."

"Aww, Honey, Monsters are not real, you see.
That's how I know that you had a bad dream."

"Mommy, please listen. The socks were there too—
All the ones that were missing, I saw it, it's true."

"Now that's it. I've had enough, Ryan!
Stop with that shouting, before you wake Bryan.

You're welcome to come and hang out in my room,
But not for too long, cause dad is coming home soon."

"No, it's okay. I'll just stay in bed.
It was just a bad dream, like you said."

Mommy left, and just like before,
That sock monster pushed open the door.

All of a sudden, Bryan called out,
"Ryan, is that what you were talking about?"

The socks and monster stood right there smiling,
And one boy was happy while the other was crying.

"I just can't believe it! You were right!
The sock monster does come out at night!"

Claudine Barbot has been writing nearly all of her life. She has a fervent love for poetry, but is passionate about all forms of expressive writing.

As a published author, Claudine already has two books in the mainstream, including "From an Officer's Wife," a poetry book detailing common experiences of police officers along with her personal experience with domestic violence and "Through a Child's Eyes," which is a children's book narrated from her young daughter's perspective about the demise of her family.

Claudine is also a playwright and an advocate for victims of domestic violence. She has been in the field of education for over a decade, but is currently pursuing writing full time.

Outside of writing, Claudine Barbot is the mother of four beautiful children and resides with them in Maryland.

Jocelyne Barbot has been writing for six years. Her specialty is fantasy, however she possesses a talent for all genres. On top of her love for penning books, she is also a playwright. By profession, Jocelyne is a Clinical Dietitian and resides in Maryland with her family.

Nicole Green McCalla has been writing for a decade. She takes pleasure in writing in all genres, but has a particular affinity to fiction. In addition to writing books, she is also a playwright.

By day, Nicole is an educator and has been in the field for over ten years. She also has two gorgeous little girls and resides in Maryland with her family.